Dear Parent:
Your child's love of rea

Every child learns to read in a differe... ...., ..., at ... or her own speed. Some go back and forth between reading levels and read favorite books again and again. Others read through each level in order. You can help your young reader improve and become more confident by encouraging his or her own interests and abilities. From books your child reads with you to the first books he or she reads alone, there are I Can Read Books for every stage of reading:

SHARED READING
Basic language, word repetition, and whimsical illustrations, ideal for sharing with your emergent reader

BEGINNING READING
Short sentences, familiar words, and simple concepts for children eager to read on their own

READING WITH HELP
Engaging stories, longer sentences, and language play for developing readers

READING ALONE
Complex plots, challenging vocabulary, and high-interest topics for the independent reader

I Can Read Books have introduced children to the joy of reading since 1957. Featuring award-winning authors and illustrators and a fabulous cast of beloved characters, I Can Read Books set the standard for beginning readers.

A lifetime of discovery begins with the magical words **"I Can Read!"**

Visit www.icanread.com for information
on enriching your child's reading experience.

I Can Read® and I Can Read Book® are trademarks of HarperCollins Publishers.

Harry at the Dog Show
Text copyright © 2023 by The Estate of Gene Zion
Illustrations copyright © 2023 by Wendy Graham Sherwood, Mindy Menschell, and Philip Clendaniel
All rights reserved. Printed in the United States of America.
No part of this book may be used or reproduced in any manner whatsoever without written permission except
in the case of brief quotations embodied in critical articles and reviews. For information address HarperCollins
Children's Books, a division of HarperCollins Publishers, 195 Broadway, New York, NY 10007.
www.icanread.com

ISBN 978-0-06-274778-5 (trade bdg.)— ISBN 978-0-06-274777-8 (pbk.)

The artist used Adobe Photoshop to create the digital illustrations for this book.

23 24 25 26 27   LB   10 9 8 7 6 5 4 3 2 1   First Edition

HARRY
at the Dog Show

Based on the character created by
Gene Zion and Margaret Bloy Graham

by Laura Driscoll with pictures by Saba Joshaghani
in the styles of Gene Zion and Margaret Bloy Graham

HARPER
An Imprint of HarperCollinsPublishers

Harry was a white dog with black spots.

He liked everything,

except … getting a bath.

Harry was glad today was not bath day.

Today was going to the park day!
The children clipped on Harry's leash
and walked down the street.

"Look, Harry!" said the little girl.

"There are so many dogs

in the park today.

They're having a dog show!"

Harry had never been to a dog show.

It looked like fun.

There were dogs everywhere!

Harry saw two friends
from his street.
He wanted to play with them
right now!
"Harry!" the little boy called.
"Wait! Stop!"

Harry ran up to his friends.

They barked and jumped.

They were so happy to see each other!

But suddenly Harry's friends
were pulled away.
And a woman pulled Harry
the other way!

"It's time for you to be groomed,"
the woman said.
"Every dog in the contest
has to be neat and clean.
Let's get you ready!"

All of a sudden,

there were people all around Harry.

One person put a green collar

on him.

Another person started fluffing
Harry's tail.

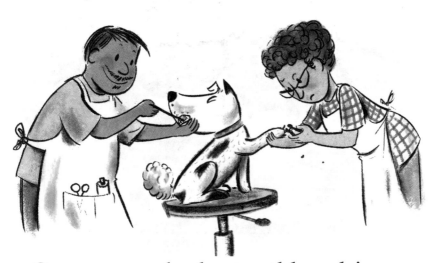

One person had a toothbrush!
Another person had nail clippers!

Then someone turned on

a blow-dryer!

It was too HOT!

Harry did not like that at all.

What was happening?

This was much worse than bath day!

He had to get away!

Harry wiggled free

and ran.

"Come back!" yelled the man

with the toothbrush.

"Come here!" yelled the woman

with the blow-dryer.

"Harry!" called the children.

"Come back here now!"

Harry had to get far, far away,

so he ran

and he dashed

and he squeezed under a fence.

Then Harry looked back.

People were still trying to catch him!

So Harry kept going.

He raced up a ramp.

He raced down a ramp.

Harry zipped across a bridge.

He jumped over a wall.

He splashed through a puddle.

Harry rushed through a tunnel
and zoomed past a woman
with a flag.

Then Harry stopped.

He looked up.

Everyone in the park

was clapping and cheering.

People were pointing at Harry.

"You did it!" "You did it!"

"You did it!" they shouted.

They were cheering for Harry!

"We have a winner!" said the woman.

"The dog with the fastest time is the

muddy white dog with black spots!"

Harry did not understand.

But then the children came running.

"You're the winner!"

said the little girl.

She gave Harry a big hug.

"You are so fast and so muddy!"

the little boy laughed.

"Let's get you home."

Harry was happy

to be back home.

He didn't even mind getting a bath

at the end of his very exciting day.